THE GREEN WISHBONE

ff

THE GREEN WISHBONE

Ruth Tomalin

Illustrated by Gavin Rowe

faber and faber
LONDON BOSTON

First published in Great Britain in 1975
by Faber and Faber Limited
3 Queen Square London WC1N 3AU
This paperback edition first published in 1989

Printed in Great Britain by
Richard Clay Ltd, Bungay, Suffolk
All rights reserved

British Library Cataloguing in Publication data is available

ISBN 0-571-15438-7

Contents

Acknowledgements

The words on the brooch (p. 37) are from Shakespeare's play *The Merchant of Venice*.

The verses on p. 80 are quoted by permission of the Literary Trustees of Walter de la Mare, and the Society of Authors as their representative, from *Now silent falls the clacking mill*, which appears in *The Complete Poems of Walter de la Mare*, published by Faber and Faber Ltd.

ONE

No animals

It wasn't a wishbone really. It was a brooch: two green enamel mistletoe leaves, and a large white pearl for a berry, set in a gold ring that had a clasp at the back and tiny writing on the front. Holly and Jon thought it was beautiful, and they called it "the green wishbone".

Mother had pinned it on today because they were moving down the hill to a new home, and she didn't want it to be lost in all the packing and unpacking.

She and Holly and Jon walked down to their new flat to wait for Dad, who would bring all their things in a van from the old home. They were going to live over a shop that sold newspapers; Mother would look after the shop all day, while Dad was at work, and Holly and Jon at school. The shop was shut today, and they sat on the stairs to the flat, waiting for the van.

It was then that Jon said dreamily, "I'll have to get up early now, won't I? Going all that way up the hill to school!"

Mother and Holly looked at one another over Jon's head. Mother said, "I did tell him . . ." and Holly, "I told him too. He just doesn't listen . . ."

So they both told him again: in the autumn, when the new term started, he wouldn't go to Hill Top Infants' School any more. He would be going to the big school just down the road—Park Road Primary School—where Holly had been for two years.

He seemed to take this in at last. Then he said, "No. I can't do that."

"Of course you can," said Mother briskly. "Why not?"

Holly knew why not. She had known all along that this change would mean trouble, if not tears. At Hill Top they kept real animals for nature study —guinea pigs and rabbits and mice; but not at Park Road. Jon would hate going to school with no animals.

Mother said, "You see, it'll be winter soon. You

won't want to walk all that way, in the rain and snow."

"I *shall* want to. All my friends are there."

"Robin and Simon? But you can still play with them! They'll come to tea on Saturdays . . ."

Jon burst out, "I hate Robin. I don't want him. He tried to lift Crispin up by his ears!"

Mother looked quite shocked. "Oh, but he mustn't! It would hurt quite a lot—poor little boy!"

"Crispin's not a boy, he's a rabbit." Jon giggled. "And Miss Brown said, if he did it again, she'd lift him up by *his* ears." He rushed on, "One boy lifted Fanny, she's a white mouse, by her tail! Only one time, though."

"Miss Brown stopped him, I hope?"

"No, Fanny did. She climbed up her own tail and bit him."

Mother said, "I see. It all sounds pretty risky to me."

The removal van drew up outside. Going down to open the door, she added, "Perhaps it's just as well you've left."

"You talk too much," Holly told him.

But at tea-time, with the flat all in order, Jon tried again.

For the first meal in their new home, they were

having a very good tea: rounds of fresh crisp bread, thickly spread with jam and clotted cream.

Jon slowly ate two slices, thinking hard. Then he suddenly asked, "Dad—you know my toy box?"

This was a large white wooden box with a guinea pig painted on the lid. Dad had made it himself for Jon's sixth birthday, so of course he knew it very well.

"I just thought," Jon said. "Can't I keep my toys in the cupboard instead?"

"And? What would you use the box for?"

Jon said gruffly, "I was thinking—perhaps—could I keep a guinea pig *in* it?"

Mother gave a loud sigh: they had had this out before. Jon cried, "Well, why *not*?"

He knew why not, but they all told him again: pets wouldn't be happy in a flat, with no garden.

And Dad said, "One day soon, I promise, we'll have our own house, and a garden too. You know we're saving up for that, as hard as we can. That's why your mother's going to work so hard, with this shop."

"So then", Mother said, "I shall have a tabby cat, and you shall have a guinea pig, and Holly can have whatever she chooses."

Holly thought, "A pony, to ride to school on." It had been her secret dream for years. She had seen some children in a TV film doing this in Australia. No one came to Park Road School on a pony: she would be the first.

Jon said quickly, "Well then! If I can't have a guinea pig here—I want to stay on at Hill Top."

Silence. Now, Holly thought, we're back at the start. Poor Jon kicked at the table leg and muttered, "I want to go to school with animals!"

Dad said, "All schools are for animals. Human animals. Boys and girls."

"I don't mean those! I mean *animal* animals!"

"No one," Dad said, "is going to school just yet. You're both off to the seaside tomorrow. Ten days at Aunt Jinny's! Had you forgotten?"

But, when tomorrow came, Jon wouldn't go. He said he would rather stay at home. No one could make him change his mind. So Dad drove Holly away in the car, to stay on her own at Aunt Jinny's by the sea.

TWO

Where Jon went

When Dad and Holly had driven off, Jon went into the shop where Mother was busy sending off the paper-boys on their rounds. He thought *he* would like to dash about in the early morning, shying papers through letter-boxes; but he wouldn't be old enough for years.

After breakfast, Mother was busy again, selling papers to people on their way to work. Jon hung about for a bit, and then said, "May I run up the hill to play with Simon?"

Simon's house was further away now, but he still needn't cross any roads to get there. So Mother said "Yes," and he set off.

But Jon had other friends at the top of the hill. And he went to see them first, with a carrot in each pocket, and a bit of toast up his sleeve.

The animals at Hill Top School lived in a big wire run in the school garden, not far from the gate. The white mice had a small cage in the run; the guinea pigs and rabbits skipped about on the grass in the day-time, and slept in safe hutches at night.

The two tortoises did not skip, or run, or even move much. They spent most of their time dozing, with their heads inside their shells. Their names—Slow and Slower—were written in chalk on the shells.

A family of baby rabbits, grey and white, had been the "stars" last term. They would play for hours, a game like leap-frog and puss-in-the-corner mixed, very funny to watch: jumping over and over each other, to and fro, flip-flop, flip-flop; until two of them jumped at the same time, bumped into each other in mid-air, and fell to the ground with a look of great surprise on their small soft faces.

But Jon's best friend was Puffball, a fluffy white guinea pig.

He had been to see her every day since the holidays began. The school gate was locked, but through the bars he could watch her running about on the grass, and could throw bits of bread, apple or carrot which now and then got through the wire mesh.

If a piece landed near the wire, Puffball would reach out with a clever paw and pull it inside.

She had a mate, Peter, but he was shy, or lazy, and spent long hours in his "burrow", a bit of hollow drain-pipe on the grass.

16

This morning, as he came near the school gate, Jon stood still for a moment in surprise. For once, the gate wasn't shut. It stood wide open, just as though term had started. A lorry was parked in the road near by, and men were going in and out of the gate, carrying planks, pots of paint and bags of tools.

Jon stood and watched. Ten minutes went by.

Now the men were all inside the school. He could hear the sound of hammering and banging in one of the class-rooms.

And still the gate stood wide open.

He looked quickly round. No one was about in the road. He slipped through the gate and ran up to the wire, calling, "Puffball! Here!"

Her white whiskery face poked out of the drain-pipe. Then she came bundling across the grass.

Jon knelt down and began to feed her with scraps of carrot. She held each bit with one paw and nibbled away. He ran to the school garden and picked a lettuce leaf for her.

How pretty she was, he thought. Her tongue looked very pink against the green leaf; like one of those little pink beans in a runner-bean pod, before you cook it. She scurried to the drain-pipe with a scrap of lettuce for Peter—then back she ran, poking her nose through the wire for Jon to stroke.

It was very hot today. The baby rabbits had grown much bigger, and seemed to have forgotten their games. They lay panting in the shade with their mother. Slow and Slower slept too, as still as hot brown stones in the sun. Even the mice were quiet. Only Puffball was wide awake, alert and gay. Jon stayed with her as long as he dared.

No one saw him run out of the gate at last, and away down the road to Simon's house.

Next morning, the gate was open again; and the

next. Jon grew so bold that he would march in, even if some of the workmen were about.

No one took any notice of him. The school keeper came in early to feed and water the animals, and again in the afternoon; but he and Jon never met.

A good many apples and carrots found their way up the hill in Jon's pockets. On Saturday the workmen were still there. He spent his pocket-money on crisps for Crispin and the other rabbits, and a ripe peach for Puffball. They both spent a blissful, sticky half-hour while she sucked at it through the wire.

Then he wiped his juicy fingers on the grass, and sat for a long time stroking her fur and tickling her ears. He felt as if she were his own pet. It would be queer, next term, having to share her again with all the others.

Next term? He had forgotten—again—about going to Park Road School.

But one day he had a shock. Mother said at tea-time, "Hasn't the time gone fast? Do you know, Holly comes back the day after tomorrow?"

Jon looked at her, and down at his plate. "But—it's still the holidays. Isn't it?"

"Only till Monday. Then back to school, both of you."

He had an odd cold feeling, as though he had

swallowed an ice whole. He whispered, "School? Hill Top?"

Mother didn't hear. She was saying, "I do wonder what Holly's been doing. I hope she hasn't been lonely—all by herself."

THREE

The pony children

Holly had been lonely for two days. Then on the third day something happened; and, when it was time to go home, she almost wished the visit need never end at all.

She was staying with Aunt Jinny, who ran a seaside guest-house and spent her time keeping her guests happy; and—much more tricky, she said—keeping the "daily helps" happy as well.

On the first morning, Holly offered to help too. This had been Mother's idea; but Aunt Jinny took it for her own, and called her an angel in human form.

"I think", Holly said, "angels always *are* in human form. In pictures they are, anyway."

"Oh! Those!" cried Aunt Jinny. "Lilies and halos and long white night-gowns—'Bright things they see, sweet harps they hold'—but could *they* grind coffee and lay the lunch tables? Tell me that!"

"*I* can," Holly said, laughing.

She loved to grind the coffee. The big coffee-mill stood on a corner of the kitchen dresser. You had to fill it up with little brown coffee beans, screw on the lid, and turn the handle 200 times. Then the beans were all gone, and you took out a glass jar of sweet-smelling brown powder—like face-powder for an African lady—ready to be spooned into the coffee-pots.

After breakfast, when the dining-room had been swept free of toast crumbs, Holly laid for lunch: six tables, with four or five places each, and a small one all to herself.

Laying the table was her job at home, so she knew how to do it properly. It didn't take long, and then she ran off to amuse herself on the beach.

All would have gone well but for a nasty little girl named Arabel, who would creep into the dining-room just before lunch and change the knives, forks and spoons about so that they were all the wrong way round. On the first day, no one saw this in time; and, as she took her place, Arabel cried at the top of her voice, "Oh, Mummee, look! Someone's been and laid the table all *wrong*!" With a gleeful smirk at Holly, who stood there blushing, unable to believe her eyes.

Luckily the trick was soon found out. Next day, Aunt Jinny had the places put right again before the lunch bell rang: all but Arabel's, which was left the wrong way round. Once more she piped, "Oh, it's laid all wrong again! Fancy not even knowing how to lay the table!" Then she saw that hers was the only one; she began to wriggle and pout.

The day after, it was the same. This time, Arabel set up a grizzle, like one of the Three Bears: "Someone's been laying *my* place all *wrong* . . . Mummee! I don't see why my place has to be the *only* one . . ." Her father and mother looked at each other—a quick, rather nervous look—and began to talk about a wasp that was zooming round the room. No doubt, Holly thought, they knew a lot about pests . . .

"That 'Orrible," the oldest daily help said later, "needs fetching a box on the ear." How Holly agreed! She would gladly have "fetched" it herself; but, after this, her neatly laid tables were left alone.

By now, anyway, she had other things to think of. She had found the pony children.

On her third morning she had paddled a long way along the beach, in and out of rocks and pools, looking at shrimps and crabs, shells and sea anemones. She still missed Jon badly and thought how much he would have liked the beach.

At last she was tired and sat down to open the surprise packet Aunt Jinny always gave her. Today it held nuts and raisins, a little cake and a green-gage.

She had this part of the beach to herself in the windy sunshine; it was nearly as nice as a desert island, she thought. But all at once there was a scrunching sound, and a troop of ponies came trotting from a pathway, across the shingle, and stopped in a circle on a wide firm stretch of sand. The ponies were ridden by boys and girls, all about Holly's age, in jeans and jerseys like hers, but with black velvet riding-caps on their heads.

A tall girl, nearly grown up, came after them riding a white horse. She seemed to be in charge;

and soon Holly understood that the boys and girls were having a lesson in riding—just as though they were in some special school where this was part of the timetable. First they did exercises: the ponies stood quite still while the riders sat bending and stretching their arms and legs, fingers and toes; it was like P.E. at school, but far more fun, Holly thought.

Next they had to walk and trot round and round, while the tall girl looked on and called out things like, "Hands down, Sandra," and, "Sit up, Clare, Michael," and once, "Felicity, your *legs*! Don't wobble about like a jelly-fish!"—which made all the children giggle.

Then the teacher made them take their feet out

of the stirrups and do all the exercises again, with the stirrups crossed over the ponies' backs in front of the saddles.

After that, they went back to walking and trotting. Then the girl said, "Canter," and some of the ponies broke into a smooth gallop, but others took no notice and went on trotting, or slowed down to a walk again, while their small riders tried to make them canter like the rest. Then they planted six flags in a ring and the ponies had to trot in and out of the flags, one by one, while the others watched and laughed; there was a lot of laughter all the time, Holly thought, though everyone was trying hard to do things right. Even the ponies seemed to be laughing.

But soon they trotted away up the shingle again, and out of sight along the path. The beach seemed very quiet and empty without them. Holly walked back to lunch in a dream, still sucking the greengage stone.

Next morning the ponies and riders were back in the same place, doing their exercises, walking, trotting, cantering and laughing. This time they had a plastic bucket full of potatoes, and at the end they took off the saddles and had potato races, three at a time.

The potatoes were laid out in rows—three rows, five potatoes in each—and the riders had to start far down the sands, ride to the first potato, jump off and pick it up, mount, ride to the bucket and drop it in; then ride back for the next potato, and so on. Then all the winners raced each other. Nobody seemed to win in the end, and nobody cared: they were all laughing too much, and so was Holly.

And they came every morning. Holly looked forward to it all the rest of the day. After lunch, Aunt Jinny always took her for a bathe, or on the pier, or up the cliff to the lighthouse; or to a film, if it rained. Nearly all the time, in secret, she was pretending to be a pony, or Holly riding a pony, or both at once.

After tea, when Aunt Jinny was cooking supper, she ran along the sea front, back to that stretch of sand. The pony children never came there in the evening; and Holly would sit astride a wooden break-water and go through the morning's lesson as though she were one of the class.

She'd never been on a pony in her life. Yet she had begun to feel that, if she ever were, she would know now just how to sit, how to hold the reins, how to keep her balance, walking, trotting, even at a canter.

If only she could really join the class. Or if only —she thought—one of the ponies would run away, and she could catch it and lead it back . . . or if only they could see her watching, and say, "Like a ride?"

27

Lucy, perhaps. Lucy had long fair plaits and long slim legs, and she always rode the same pony, Catkin; he was cream-coloured, with a dark mane and tail. Sometimes the teacher said, "Good, Lucy," when they were doing exercises. Holly couldn't see why, any more than she could see what was wrong with other people's hands, or feet, or knees, to make the teacher call out to them by name, half shocked, half smiling. Holly only knew that, if ever her chance came, she would try to ride like Lucy. She *knew* she could do it!

But how could she get to know them? No pony ran away. No one ever looked at Holly. They were kept far too busy to notice a girl sitting by herself on the break-water.

And the holiday was racing by. A week was gone in a flash: soon it would be the sad last day. She would go home and never see the pony children again.

The last day came; but it wasn't sad at all. Later, Holly thought: the best day of my life, so far.

FOUR

Really riding

That morning she had seen the pony class as usual.
When they rode away up the path, she turned and
ran, not wanting to see them go for the last time.

After tea, Aunt Jinny said, "I expect you'll want
to go and say good-bye to the sea." Holly nodded.
There wouldn't be time in the morning, she knew,
as Dad was coming very early, so as to go to work
when he'd driven her home.

So she set off. She didn't go on the beach, but
ran along the sea front, on and on, till she came once
again to the path that the pony children used. Suddenly she had made up her mind: she would try
to find out where the ponies came from. Why
hadn't she thought of that before?

The path went up among green bushes to the
top of a cliff, where it came out into a road with
houses on each side. Holly went straight on.
Quite soon the road turned into a lane, running between trees and hedges. She seemed to have run
a mile, and was nearly out of breath, when she

heard voices in a field some way ahead. She knew one of the voices: it was Lucy's. Only that morning she'd heard her chattering to Clare as they waited their turn in "bending" practice.

Holly stopped dead, then tiptoed on, and up to a gate.

There were three people in the field: Lucy, riding Catkin; an older girl, Tina, riding a black pony named Skippy; and a boy, Jeff. Holly found out their names within a few minutes as they called to one another.

Lucy and Tina were taking turns at jumping their mounts over some low fences, made of gorse and bracken, set in the middle of the field. Catkin sailed over each jump, but Tina was having trouble: Skippy would stop short, or swerve to one side, at the last minute.

When he had done this three or four times, Jeff said what sounded like—"We need wings." Holly thought of Aunt Jinny's angels, and smiled to herself. And just at that moment the miracle happened. Lucy looked round, caught sight of Holly by the gate, trotted over and said gently, "Hello. Like to come and be a wing?"

It had come at last: but so quickly that Holly was taken completely by surprise. She nearly turned and bolted in sheer panic. But she found herself climbing over the gate, walking towards

the fences, just as she might have done in one of her daydreams.

Jeff said, "That's fine. Come and stand here, will you? Like this." He led her to the first fence and made her stand beside it, arms stretched out; then he stood facing her at the other end of the fence.

Now Holly found herself shivering: not with fear —though, all of a sudden, the ponies looked *huge*, all legs and hard-shod feet—but with shock. Could this really be happening?

Here came Lucy and Catkin: she stood firm. Over they went, and landed lightly on the other side of the fence. You could see Catkin loved to jump.

Now Skippy . . . Tina put him straight for the middle of the fence. He laid back his ears, looking angry. He was all set to pull up, or to swerve to one side and bolt: but he couldn't; he was going too fast, and there were the wings, Holly and Jeff, arms wide, to block his escape. He was over before he knew what had happened.

He gave a wild snort and flew on, over the next jump, and the last. Jeff cheered.

Tina rode on, calling, "Going in now. I think he's had enough." She waved and trotted away down the field.

Holly was backing away, but Lucy stopped her.

"Your turn now," she said, sliding off Catkin.

Holly stammered, "Oh, I can't. I can't ride. I've never learnt."

Lucy said, "That's all right. Have a try on Catkin. Look, put your foot here. That's it. Now jump. Up you go."

And there she was, in the saddle, her feet in the stirrups; and Lucy was showing her how to hold the reins.

"That's fine. Now we'll walk. All right? Just to see if you like it . . ." said Lucy kindly.

If she liked it!

Holly felt herself going pink in the face; then very pale. It was too much. Dreams should never come true like this, all in a moment, before you had

time even to think . . . while your head was spinning, your knees trembling, your mouth too dry to let you say a word.

And where was that Holly who used to envy the riders, and feel so sure she could do it right away, if only she had the chance?

But Lucy held the bridle; they were moving, walking down the edge of the field. Catkin's head bobbed in front of her; his neck was arched, his ears pricked up. She felt his four legs moving strongly and steadily. And all at once she found her balance and began to enjoy herself. At the end of the field she put out her hand to pat the warm smooth neck, to feel the crisp mane. Lucy turned and smiled.

"You're doing fine. Shall we trot a bit? Hold on to the saddle in front if you like!"

Holly was going to cry, "No!" But there wasn't time. Lucy broke into a gentle trot, Catkin did the same. Holly found herself bumping in the saddle, gritting her teeth, biting her tongue . . . she was going to call out, "Stop, stop, stop . . ." but another miracle happened. Again she found her balance. The bumping had stopped. Catkin was still trotting, and Holly was sitting up straight, heels down, feet firm in the stirrups, while she rose and fell gently in time with the pony's gentle pace. She was really riding . . .

Me, she thought: Holly: I'm riding, like the pony children.

Then it was over. They were back at the fences. Lucy helped her to jump down. Jeff strolled up and said rather grandly, "I say. If that was your first time, you did jolly well."

"Yes," said Lucy, "she did."

They both smiled, pleased with her. She stood stroking Catkin's nose, suddenly hearing herself gasp out, "I've seen you on the beach, in the mornings. You"—she told Lucy—"and all those others."

"Oh, have you? Well—come and have a ride tomorrow."

She had really said that.

Later—dawdling back along the sea front, with the breeze cooling her face, the grey tide lapping and whispering far away down the sands, the gulls crying their sad cries—she remembered: tomorrow she would be gone.

Never mind. She had ridden a pony, walking and trotting. Tomorrow she would tell Jon about it.

Ever since she'd said good-bye and left the field, Holly had been moving softly and quietly, like someone walking in her sleep, trying not to wake. Now, all in a moment, delight broke over her like a great wave, fresh and dazzling.

She jumped down on to the beach and raced up and down the bright wet sands, flying over the break-waters. Going home to Aunt Jinny's, she sang all the way.

FIVE

One wish each

It was a funny thing. Holly and Jon had meant to tell each other all about their secret doings, as soon as they met again. But when Holly came home, both found they didn't want to tell just yet. Holly wanted to keep quiet about the ponies, and think about it all when she was alone. Jon was afraid she might say he mustn't visit Hill Top School any more, now that he had left. So he would never see Puffball again.

They talked about other things: but each knew the other had a secret.

When Holly came to bed, the first night after her return, she found Jon wide awake, sitting on his bed and looking at something on the palm of his hand. He shut his fingers over it quickly, but Holly had seen a gleam of green and white in the dusk. She cried, "You've got the green wishbone!"

"Shhhhh! They'll hear!"

"You took it out of Mother's drawer! Hurry up and put it back." But it wasn't much use being

36

bossy in a whisper: Jon took no notice, except to hiss again, "Shhhh," and then—

"Come and look. I want to show you . . ."

He opened his fingers, and they both looked at the brooch: the two green leaves, the shining pearl, the gold pin.

He pointed to the tiny letters on the lower curve of the ring. "D'you *see*? It says, *you can wish!* I never saw that before!"

"Well, you couldn't *read* before." Holly put her finger-nail on the upper curve. "There's a lot more, do you see? It starts up here—that bit you read is the end. It says—*I wish you all the joy that* . . . and then your bit . . . *you can wish*."

Jon read it over in a whisper: " 'I wish you all the joy that you can wish.' "

There was a silence. At last he breathed, "It's . . . not really a wishbone, is it? Can it give wishes?"

"It's not a wishbone at all. It just looks like one. It's a sprig of mistletoe . . ."

But, as she said this, Holly thought of a lesson about Druids, and a picture of fierce-looking men, in long white robes and long white beards, cutting mistletoe from oak trees. *They* had thought it was magic. The book said so.

Watching her face in the dusk, Jon whispered:

"If someone gave you three wishes—what would you wish?"

37

Holly whispered back, "Shouldn't need three. One would do."

"Yes. Me too."

Jon held up the brooch. The pearl berry caught the last light from the west. It shone like a tiny lamp. He breathed, "One wish each?"

Holly nodded. "And we mustn't tell. Not even each other."

When you wish on a chicken wishbone, you pull till it breaks into two pieces, and the one with the longer piece is the lucky one. Of course, they couldn't break the mistletoe brooch. They each put a finger on it, and shut their eyes; their lips moved silently.

"I wish I had ponies to ride."

"I wish to go to school with animals. *Animal* animals."

They hadn't made a sound for half a minute. Perhaps the strange hush made itself felt in the sitting-room, along the passage. They heard Dad say something. Then Mother's voice:

"Holly! Are you in bed yet?"

Holly snatched the brooch, tiptoed into Mother's room, slid it into the drawer, tiptoed back and sang out:

"Yes."

Under her breath she added, "Nearly," and tore off her jersey.

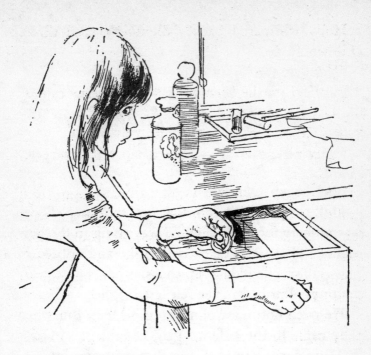

The spell was broken.

Jon wriggled and yawned under his blanket. Holly tipped sand from her shoes and thought glumly:

"Stupid. There aren't any ponies here. So what's the use of wishing?"

SIX

Jon at school

School began two days later.

Holly was to take Jon, that first morning. There was no help for it, he saw: he was going to the new school. They set out early, bright and spruce in new pullovers and lace-up shoes.

Only—Jon had never felt less bright.

He tried not to sulk and drag his feet. But when they came to the Infants' gate he said:

"Don't come in with me. I want to go by myself."

"But you don't know where to go! Let me just——"

"*No*, I tell you." He looked through the gate. A small crowd of children had already come, waiting for the doors to open. "I can wait with *them*," Jon pointed out.

The Infants' School wasn't part of the Junior block where Holly went: it stood on its own, cut off by a wooden fence. Holly knew she wouldn't see Jon again, to speak to, for the rest of the day—not till she reached home that afternoon. Would he really be all right? She said slowly:

"You're sure you don't mind . . . ?" About coming here, she meant. *After all the fuss you made*, she was too kind to add. Jon saw the words in her face, and said bitterly:

"Don't tag on to me. I'm not a baby. I've been to school for *years*!"

Holly wanted to find her own new class and have a game with her friends before the bell rang. She said, "Well. Good-bye, then."

He turned his back and marched through the gate.

Holly watched him go. But only for a moment; if he turned and saw her watching, he might still change his mind and make a scene, she knew. Only *she* understood how near he had been to one, ever since he woke this morning.

Jon looked back and saw she was gone. He walked more slowly. It seemed miles and miles of open space, between him and the crowd at the glass doors. He felt like a small fly crawling over a huge white table-cloth.

It was worse when he came near the others; they turned and stared at him. He wished he'd let Holly come, after all. He dug his hands into his trouser pockets, and found a carrot he'd put there when no one was looking, just in case he had a chance to get to Hill Top.

41

It made him feel much worse. He thought of his old playground, full of boys and girls now, all looking at the animals, giving them titbits, telling the new children their names. It wasn't fair. Puffball would be missing him.

"Why are you making faces?" a cool voice asked.

Jon looked at the speaker: a tall girl, older than Holly, holding two much smaller ones by the hand: you could see they were just starting school, Jon thought, and that girl had come with them. But *he* hadn't needed anyone; he was only new *here*. He drew himself up and tried to keep his face in order.

But that girl still eyed him with a sharp mocking look. She knew quite well he'd been near to tears. He dug his finger-nails into the carrot; then drew out his hand to flip the bits of yellow carrot from under his nails, as if he were too busy to notice her.

She let go of the two small hands, took a quick step up to Jon and said, teasingly, "What has it got in its pockets?" Before he could stop her, she whisked out the carrot and held it up.

"Oh look—a carrot! Is that your lunch? You must be a little donkey—are you?"

She held it out, daring him to snatch: if he did, she would easily dodge him. Already she had the others laughing.

Jon kept his head, put his hands back in his

pockets and strolled away from the group, round the corner of the school, out of sight.

No one came after him.

There were trees and shrubs at the back of the school. With a swift look round, in case of prying eyes, he slipped in among them and came to the back fence. Not stopping to think, he climbed a tree and dropped over the fence into the road. If you walked along it, he knew, you came to Bell Hill, and that led to Hill Top. He set off at a run.

The bell trilled out as he came to the well-known

gate. Slipping into the cloakroom, hanging his wind-cheater on his old peg, he felt happy for the first time that day.

School was full of his friends. "Look," they said, "here's old Jon. Nearly late as usual. Hello, Jon."

Simon said, "Thought you told us you weren't coming?"

Jon said nothing to this.

"Didn't he, Rob? He *said*——"

A teacher swooped down on them, and Simon forgot all about it.

Jon wished he could forget. All day, as he joined in lessons and games and dinner and singing, he was filled by turns with dread, and with triumph. Here he was, just where he'd wanted to be: it had been so easy. And yet—he knew he'd done something wicked. He *must* have. At any moment someone might come to the class-room door and say in a terrible voice, "Where's Jon Gale? Fetch him out. He's not at this school any more."

Two things helped him, he saw. Their beloved Miss Brown had left, and the top class had a new teacher; and also, someone had measles, or their brother had measles, and couldn't come back yet. So the numbers were right: he didn't know what he would have done if there had been a table and chair short.

Also, of course, the new teacher didn't know

anyone yet by name. They all had to stand up one by one while she read the names from the register, to see who was who. Robin and Simon tried to swap names, but the rest giggled so much that she soon saw what was going on. In all the first-day bustle, no one noticed that Jon's name was never called at all.

After dinner he had a very bad moment. He was at the wire, stroking Puffball, when the Head herself, Miss Tee, came by and stopped.

"Why, hello, Jon! Are you paying us a visit?"

He stood up, feeling that all was lost, he must fly: but his legs were trembling too much. He could only stand there, waiting for his doom.

But she only smiled, "I see. You've come up to look at the animals?" She moved away, saying kindly, "Don't be late back to school, will you?"

Nothing else happened. He could hardly believe his luck. If he had planned the whole thing, it couldn't have worked out better. The afternoon slid past, and he was still there. For Nature, they took the new teacher out to see the animals and told her all about them. Then it was time to go home.

He ran down the hill as fast as he could go; and now he was filled with dread once more, for something *must* have happened while he was away. Suppose they'd come to tell Mother he was missing? Suppose Holly got home first and saw him coming the wrong way?

But still nothing happened. All went well. Mother was upstairs, getting tea ready, waiting to ask:

"Did you like school?"

"Yes, I did." Well, it was true: he'd had a lovely day—but for the bad moments, and they hadn't lasted long.

Holly came in, sharper-eyed than Mother, full of questions. "How did you get on? I looked through the fence at dinner-time, I couldn't see you anywhere."

"I know. I hid. I don't want you looking out for me."

"But where were you, then?"

"I went round the back, where those bushes are."

"Oh." That sounded all right. Holly went off to change.

He'd never known it was so easy to trick people; but deep down a small voice told him that he wasn't really being clever.

He took no notice. He'd had one whole day at Hill Top. Next day could look after itself.

But the next day came; and still it went on being easy. He said good-bye to Holly at the school gate, waited for her to go, ran round to the back, climbed the tree and slipped over the fence. He had to run as fast as he could, not to be late at Hill Top: they hadn't set out so early this morning. He came in behind the last stragglers and took his place in class.

Today, he told himself, he must keep out of sight of Miss Tee, the Head. So long as she didn't see him, he might never be found out. He might stay on till he was seven, like all the rest. If only he could dodge Miss Tee; and if Holly didn't begin to suspect; and if no one at Park Road found out . . . It seemed a lot to hope for, after all.

He didn't enjoy today quite so much, because all these thoughts made him shiver from time to time. But, for Nature, they went out and filled a box with straw for the tortoises to sleep in, through the winter. That cheered him up again.

The week went on. Still, by turns, he was happy and scared. But he was still there.

Then came the fifth morning. Black Friday.

As they were trooping out to play, the teacher said, "You're Jon Gale, aren't you? It's funny, but your name doesn't seem to have got itself on my register!"

His face burned. She laughed and said:

"You needn't look so upset. *I* know you're here. So we'd better write you down, hadn't we?"

And she wrote his name at the bottom of the list. It was as simple as that!

47

He skipped out into the playground, laughing to himself because it *had* been so simple, after all: now that he could answer to his name, like the others, he felt he was really back at school, and safe. He spread out his arms like a jet plane, skimmed off the run-way and screamed up into the blue sky, faster and faster.

And dived right into Miss Tee, on one of her little strolls round the playground.

The jet plane came down to earth with a crash. She gasped at the bump, and held him by the arm, saying crisply, "Now, Jon! Try to look where you're going."

He gulped, muttered, "Yes, Miss Tee," and made to rush away. But she still held his arm, and gave him a long, thoughtful look. A puzzled look. She said:

"You here *again*, Jon?"

Of course he'd known it would have to come. Here it was: he was found out. Miss Tee knew he'd really left. And just how bad was the thing he'd done? What was Dad going to say when he heard, and Mother, and Holly?

But he was saved for the moment. Someone came running up in a hurry: a young lady from the school office.

"Oh, Miss Tee, you're wanted on the 'phone. A Miss Mouncey. Very urgent, she said——"

Miss Tee let go of Jon. At once, a pair of robbers —Robin and Simon—swooped to the rescue and whisked him off in their get-away car.

When he was able to look back, the Head was walking away, the other lady chattering at her side. And as they went in, Jon was sure he heard the fatal words: "From Park Road School."

He thought about that for the rest of the morning. He couldn't read, or write, or draw.

And at twelve o'clock, when the office lady came to his class-room at last with the message—"Will Jon Gale go to Miss Tee, please?"—there was no Jon to answer. His chair was empty. He wasn't in the cloakroom, or in the playground. He had slipped away.

SEVEN

Where Holly went

Term started smoothly for Holly. She didn't forget the pony children; but she was too busy to think of them much, for the first two days at least.

She did think Jon was very quiet: but not really unhappy. He wouldn't talk about school, and it seemed best to let him alone. He'd soon get to like it, Holly thought.

After school, Mother was busy again in the shop, selling the evening papers. Holly and Jon changed into jeans, had tea in the kitchen, and then went out to play in the park at the top of the road.

But on Wednesday afternoon they stayed in the flat, watching something that Holly had found by chance on television: young riders jumping in a horse show. Jon looked and drew rabbits by turns; but Holly couldn't take her eyes off the horses.

She was very cross when Mother came up and told them to run out into the fresh air while they had the chance.

"Plenty of time to watch television, when the dark evenings come."

"Oh, do let me stay a minute! Oh, look, here's another one going to jump——" Holly put her hand over the switch; she wouldn't turn it off, and in the end she rushed downstairs in a raging temper, leaving Jon to trail after her.

When they came to the park, he went to the roundabout, as usual. There was a swing empty, but Holly didn't grab it. She dawdled back to the park entrance, muttering, "Stupid silly swings, stupid silly slide, stupid boring old park, *nothing* to do."

There was a bus-stop at the entrance. Just as she got there, a bus drew up. Before she had made up her mind, Holly found she had jumped on, run up the stairs, and thrown herself down in an empty seat in front. The bell rang; the bus sailed off down the street.

She had never been in a bus by herself. But no one had ever said she mustn't. Of course she knew one must never go in a car, except with Dad, and never talk to strangers. But a bus conductor didn't seem to count. She had a 5p piece in her pocket; when he came round she gave it to him, and he said, "Wild Apple Gate?" and handed her a ticket.

She knew now which way the bus was going:

over the moor, to the town where Dad drove to work every day. She had been there twice with him, and she knew Wild Apple Gate was the name of a place at the top of the moor, with a little shop at the roadside. She could enjoy the bus ride there, and then come back on the next bus, and pick up Jon at the park, and no one would know.

What about the fare back? Well, that would be all right, too. For, in the pocket of her jeans, she still had two bright 50p pieces that Aunt Jinny had given her: her wages for the coffee-grinding and table-laying. And Aunt Jinny had said:

"Now tell Dad and Mother that's not for your money-box. It's for you to spend, on something you really want."

She had meant to tell them this when she got home; and she hadn't exactly forgotten, yet the money was still hidden in her pocket. A whole pound: far more than she'd ever had before. To spend just as she liked.

The streets and houses were left behind. The bus had climbed up to Hill Top and down the other side. Now they were going up another long hill to the moor. A breeze came through the open window. Holly had long ago stopped feeling cross. She was only sorry she had left Jon behind in the park. He loved riding on bus-tops as much as she did herself.

The bell rang: the conductor called, "Wild Apple Gate!"

When the bus was gone, there was no one in sight: only the little shop beside the road, and beyond it the wide moor, the purple heather and green gorse.

A few twisted wild crab trees grew by the ditch, with yellow leaves and tiny green apples. A robin sang among the red hips on a briar bush. The sun was in the west, the sky full of soft pink light.

Holly was glad she had come. But what about a bus back? There was the bus-stop, over the road. She'd better cross over and wait, in case she missed the next one. . . .

Then her money chinked in her pocket. It would be nice to have some sweets to crunch while she was waiting: and she could ask about the bus times in the shop.

But when she came near the shop door, Holly forgot all about sweets, and buses. She forgot everything—except a big white sign on a board at the door. She stood there and read it over and over.

The sign said, in tall black letters on a white board:

PONY
RIDES
5P

53

At last she pushed open the door and went in.

The front part of the shop had a counter with packets of sweets, and an ice-box. Behind this, Holly saw a tea-room with glass walls and rows of tables. Through the glass wall at the back, she saw a strip of garden, and a white gate into a field.

An old lady sat knitting on a chair behind the counter. In a fawn jacket and skirt, and bright red jumper, she looked like a robin. A black cat lay across her knees, and a large dog across her feet.

She blinked as though she'd been dozing; perhaps she could knit in her sleep?

"Well," she said, "I was just going to shut the shop. Now, what will you have?"

Holly whispered, "A pony ride, please."

She had to say it again, much louder, and point to the board outside: and still the old lady seemed taken aback.

"A ride? Well, I'm not sure . . . are you all by yourself?"

"Yes. I came on the bus. I'm going back on the next one, down the hill."

"Are you? Then you've only"—she looked at her watch—"only twenty minutes . . ."

"One ride", Holly said bravely, "wouldn't take as long as that?" She put one of the 50p pieces on the counter. Three pairs of eyes stared at her— bright brown, green, yellow. She stared back.

There was a long pause. Suddenly the old lady smiled, put down her knitting and tried to get up. Now the green and the yellow eyes looked up at her in dismay. The cat dug its claws into her lap; the dog gave a groan. But she shook them off and stood up, rubbing her knees and trying out her feet, as though they'd given her pins-and-needles.

She said slowly, still thinking things over:

"The pony rides—they were really for the tea-room customers, you see. My son thinks it's good for children to have the chance of a ride. Nowadays —all these cars and planes, you know . . . they're not the same for children . . ."

Holly said, "I *know*." And something in her voice seemed to please the old lady. She smiled and became quite brisk: leading the way through the tea-room, with Holly close behind, and the cat and dog following.

They came out into the garden and went down the path to the white gate. There was the field; and four ponies grazing. The old lady picked up a bowl with some corn in it and began to call, "Coop, coop—Boxer, Dobbin, Prince."

Three of the ponies stopped eating grass, eyed the bowl and moved nearer the gate. The fourth took no notice, but went on munching grass.

Holly found herself gaz-
ing at a big notice by the gate:

The old lady shook her head—"Oh yes—we had to put that up in the summer. Some rather rough boys came up from the town and —wait! You have to stand under the mark."

The white pole that held

the notice had a black ring near the top. Holly stood with her back to the pole; the top of her head came inches below the black mark. The old lady smiled again.

"Some of the boys and girls who come are quite big. At first we said the rides were for under-twelves, but then it would be, 'Oh, miss, I'm only ten, I'm big for my age'—so now we let them ride if they're not too tall."

She turned to the gate, shaking the corn in the bowl. Three pony heads were now hanging over the bars. The fourth pony tossed his head and moved further off. But one eye was still towards the gate; and the old lady laughed.

"That's Lion, over there. We have to be careful, and keep the gate shut—he's just on the look-out for a chance to nip through and run off to the farm."

Holly thought she would love to ride Lion. He was cream-coloured, like Catkin, but darker. The other ponies were dusty, rust-coloured, shaggy and plump: Lion was sleek.

His owner said, "We named them after the farm horses, you know." Her voice sounded quiet and far away for a moment.

"Four plough horses we had, when I was your age. Boxer, Dobbin, Prince and Lion. We've only a tractor now, of course."

She sighed.

Then her voice changed. "Now! Shall I lead you? I'm not a very quick walker, as you see."

"Oh no, thank you! I can go by myself!"

"But—have you ever ridden before?"

"Yes, I have," Holly told her firmly. "Walking *and* trotting."

"Well! Suppose you take Dobbin. He's very good, he'll look after you."

Dobbin—Holly was rather glad to see—was the smallest of the three. He was also the plumpest and shaggiest. The old lady shoo'ed the other two away, and let Dobbin put his head in the corn bowl, while Holly climbed the gate. From the top bar, it was easy to slide on to the warm furry back. Dobbin was still, only letting his skin ripple softly as though she were a fly.

The old lady let go of the halter. Holly sat there, so filled with bliss that she could hardly breathe.

Dobbin had no saddle or bridle, only the rope halter, and a strap round his neck. Holly put one hand on the strap, and stroked the rough mane with the other. She sat up straight, thinking of Lucy, and clicked her tongue.

Nothing happened: Dobbin didn't move until the lady spoke to him.

"Go on, there—go on at once, sir," she told him, and waved him away from the gate.

He began to walk up the field. Holly felt cool air on her ankles, as his feet went swishing through rushes and grass. She chanted softly, "Dobbin, Dobbin," and saw his ears twitch back to listen. She patted his neck with her free hand.

At the top of the field he turned in a wide circle and made for the gate, a little faster, but still at a walk. Holly pressed her feet against his sides, and clicked her tongue again. This time he seemed to hear; he broke into a trot.

This took her by surprise; but only for a moment. She gasped, hung on to the neck-strap with both hands and tried with all her might to sit firmly, not to slide about. In the distance she saw those three faces watching her: the lady, the cat and the dog.

It felt so bumpy, she couldn't get her breath: and suddenly it wasn't bumpy, after all. She was really riding, again: as she'd done on Catkin. She could still do it.

Then it was over. They were back at the fence, Dobbin putting out his nose to the corn bowl. But the lady waved him away again, calling:

"Off you go—three times up and down the field —Dobbin, you know that very well, sir!"

So it wasn't over yet.

Twice more they walked up the field and trotted back, in a blur of green grass, yellow hedges, mauve September flowers, late sunlight. The third time, as she came near, the lady called:

"Your bus! You'll have to hurry. Quick—there —run!" She pressed the 50p piece back into Holly's hand, as she slid off the gate.

"But I haven't paid you!" Holly gasped.

"Never mind, never mind—no time to look for change!" She pointed to the road. Far away over the moor, Holly saw the tall red bus. It was moving fast. She had just time to run through the garden, through the shop door, to look both ways, cross the road and dart along to the bus-stop. She did remember to call, "Thank you!" and heard a faint call in reply:

"Come again."

Then the bus roared up. She rushed up the stairs and found a seat at the back, by the window. But just as she sat down, the conductor was at her side, frowning at the 50p piece, counting out the change very slowly, mostly in 2p pieces.

By the time she was free to look, the shop was out of sight. They were far down the hill, with the town rushing to meet them.

Soon the bus stopped outside the park. Jon had run back to supper. Holly went home in one of her dreams, still trotting down the field in the pink sunset light; still hearing that faint call, "Come again," and the "huffle" of a pony.

Going upstairs to the flat, stuffing the handful of secret money into one of her winter socks at the back of a drawer, she thought:

"I *must* go again, anyway. I didn't pay her!"

EIGHT

Milk with Miss Mouser

That was on Wednesday.

As soon as she woke on Thursday morning, Holly thought, "I'll go there again, after school!" And so she did.

Again, it was a beautiful evening; with a blue sky full of little pink clouds, the robin singing, the wild crab apples hanging in the hedge like strings of green beads.

She rode Dobbin; while the others ate grass, and Lion kept one eye on the gate.

When she slid back into the garden, fishing in her jeans pocket for those five 2p pieces to pay for two rides, the old lady said, "What a pity we're closing so soon."

Holly thought she meant, closing for the night. But she had to run for the bus again—there wouldn't have been time for a second ride. Perhaps on Saturday? On Saturday she might get away in the morning . . .

Sailing back on top of the bus, her head was full

of plans. She was going to ride at Wild Apple Gate for ever and ever: at least, until she got too tall, and her head came up to the black mark. When Aunt Jinny's pound was gone, she would earn some more. How soon would Mother let her do a paper-round?

Then came Friday.

When Holly's class went out to mid-morning break, Miss Mouncey, who ran the school office, was lying in wait at her door. This lady was known as Miss Mouser, because of her cat-like ways; and as Holly went by, she pounced, waving a sheaf of papers.

"Holly Cole? You've a little brother, haven't you? John Cole?"

Holly nodded. If Miss Mouser said your name was Cole, not Gale, it would be quicker to agree. On the first day of term, she'd pounced on Holly just like this, "to check the new address"; which she said was Parker Street, getting quite cross when Holly said that it was Park Road. In the end, Holly had missed a lot of break.

What did she want to know today? Something about a *note*? "We don't seem to have had any note from your mother?"

Jerked from thoughts of Dobbin and Lion, Holly said quickly, "Oh, Mother's busy in the shop now." She meant to be helpful; but Miss Mouser's nose twitched, her tawny eyes sparked, as though she'd heard this sort of thing once too often.

"We should have had the note *at once*. Even if your mother is busy!"

She fixed Holly with a stern gaze and added:

"Do you think he'll be well enough to start on Monday?"

Holly looked lost. "Who will——?"

"Your brother, of course! James"—she looked at the sheaf of papers—"John Cole? The child who's away with 'flu?"

"*Jon?* But—he started *last* Monday! He's here *now*!"

Miss Mouser's nose grew pink. She ruffled through her papers and asked, "Now, what makes you say that?"

"He comes with me. Every day." (Half of break gone already, nearly!) "I see him to the gate. You know—the Infants," said Holly, speaking slowly and clearly, as she sometimes spoke to Jon himself. "He came with me today."

But still Miss Mouser didn't let her go. Looking more ruffled than her papers, she gazed at Holly and said, in a queer small voice:

"Oh dear . . ."

A sudden chill of fear struck at Holly. *Could* Jon have been taken ill? So far he'd never had 'flu in his life!

64

And she'd seen him, two hours ago, padding into the Infants.

Then why was Miss Mouser looking at her like that? With a sort of greedy gleam, like a cat with a mouse *and* a dish of cream?

At Holly's stricken look, the gleam vanished. Miss Mouser purred, "Never mind . . ." and, with another swift pounce, she had Holly by the wrist, drew her into the office and shut the door.

There was a pan of milk on a gas ring by the fire. Miss Mouser lit the gas, took two mugs from a shelf, put Holly into a chair and gave her a mug of warm milk.

"Now. Drink that. Nothing to worry about."

Then why did she ask, so sweetly, after taking one sip from her own mug:

"Has he ever stayed away from school before?"

"Stayed away? Only with one of his tummy aches." But that, she saw, was the wrong answer.

"Drink your milk," said Miss Mouser's purring voice; but her eyes had a sly look. No; not quite sly. A *thinking* look. And—could she be . . . a bit scared? Panic swept over Holly. But now Miss Mouser smiled, as though she knew exactly what to do, at last.

She began to ruffle the papers again. "Now, where was he at school before? St. Paul's, wasn't it?"

"Hill Top," Holly said. "And he's not John Cole," she added. "He's Jon Gale." And she burst into tears.

"Oh *dear* . . ." said Miss Mouser; as if to say, "Now we *are* in trouble."

Holly put down her empty mug and fled. As the office door shut behind her, she heard the tinkle of a 'phone being taken off. Then a moment later, "Hill Top School? Miss Tee, please . . . Yes. It's urgent."

So now the 'phone wires hummed between Park Road and Hill Top: and soon it had all come out.

First there was Miss Mouser, very smooth, saying:

66

"Oh, Miss Tee. About a child you had last year. James—no, Jon, Jon Gale . . ."

As she said this, there was a little laugh from the other end of the 'phone. Miss Mouser's tone grew sharp, to show it was not a laughing matter:

"Can you tell me—is there any *history* of *truancy*?" That was a rather uppish way of asking, as she'd just asked Holly: "Has he ever stayed away from school before?"

But Miss Tee laughed again. "Jon? Never. In fact—just the other way. I find we've still got him here."

Then Miss Tee told Miss Mouser how fond Jon was of the school animals; and they both laughed and clicked their tongues.

"Strictly speaking," Miss Tee said, "this couldn't happen here. We'd have spotted him at once, as a rule. Only, with new staff—and all these measles cases——"

"Of course!" cried Miss Mouser. "And it could never have happened with *us*—not for a single day —but with so much summer 'flu—so many new children absent——"

The wires went on humming away, while the two ladies told each other why something that could *never* happen, had happened: so that Jon had been at the wrong school for nearly a week, without being found out.

At last—"Well," said Miss Tee, "we'll keep him here for the rest of the day."

But there, of course, she was wrong. Just as Miss Mouser was wrong when she said, "I shan't forget to tell his sister he's with you."

NINE

Tea with Miss Tee

When Holly dashed out of Miss Mouser's office, she knew something was amiss. Something to do with Jon.

She ran out of doors and over to the fence that shut off the Junior playground from the squeaks of the Infants on the other side.

She had peered through a crack each day, looking for Jon; but he had never been in sight. Nor was he now. And already break was over.

She had to brush away tears and smears from her face, and go in with her class. She had been looking forward to the next lesson. In the time-table it was called Natural Science, which seemed very grown-up; and it was with a new master.

It turned out to be about Seeds, and the master handed round all kinds for the class to look at: conkers in their shells, sweet chestnuts in their hedgehog prickles, acorns in acorn-cups, an apple cut in half, thistle-down, dandelion clocks. Just like our old Nature lessons, Holly thought.

But, whatever the lesson was called, she heard very little of it. She was far too unhappy about Jon.

It was the same with the next lesson, when they had to write about the week's doings in their Friday newsbooks. Holly couldn't write about Wild Apple Gate, as that was a secret; and her latest news was far too bad to write.

For, all of a sudden, she saw it all. Jon was playing truant, she thought. That was what Miss Mouser had been talking about. He must have been doing it all the week: slipping off as soon as she left him alone. He'd never been to school at all!

But then—what had he been doing? Where had he been, and where was he now?

At last the bell rang for the end of the morning. Out went the teacher; in came the rich brown smell of Friday's dinner, fish-and-chips and ginger pudding. But Holly couldn't wait for dinner.

Find Jon! she thought. That's the first thing.

Where could she start to look? What could he have done with himself, day after day, all alone? And without any dinner?

Could he—*could* he have just gone home, got into the flat when Mother wasn't looking, and hidden there all day? Under his bed, perhaps?— slipping out now and then to steal a crust or a biscuit?

70

She didn't really think this likely. Better make sure, though. She ran down Park Road.

The street door to the flat was locked. She had to go in by the shop: how could *he* have done that, without being seen? In the dinner-hour, the shop was full of grammar school boys and girls; but of course Mother spotted Holly at once, and cried, "Hello, there. What a nice surprise!"

Mother added, smiling, "I was just wishing you two could come in!"

She had just been wishing . . . and there, pinned to her shirt, Holly saw the green wishbone. She put up a finger and touched it: "I wish to find Jon. Quickly. Oh, please . . ."

But he was not in the flat. She ran from room to room, looking under beds, in cupboards, behind curtains. No Jon.

Outside again, she began to walk slowly away— but where to? A tall red-haired lady was coming up to the shop. They saw each other at the same time.

"Oh! Miss Tee!"

"Holly!"

Then, both at once—"Jon!"

And Holly gasped, "He's been with you? At Hill Top?"

But Miss Tee said, "Yes, he was—but not now. He's run home. I must go and explain to your mother."

71

"No!" Holly cried. "He's not there. Oh, don't tell Mother yet. I"—she had a bright idea—"I'm just going up to the park, I think he's gone there to play."

"Then", said Miss Tee, exactly like Henny Penny, "I shall go with you."

Her red mini car was parked near by. A moment later, Holly was sitting beside Miss Tee, spinning up Park Road. At any other time, she would have felt as though the sky were really falling. It was almost like being asked to drive with the Queen. But she was far too upset to feel pleased and proud.

She was still more upset when they got to the park: there was no sign of Jon there either. She was close to tears again. But Miss Tee said:

"Come along. He can't be far off. We'll drive about a bit. . . ."

He was not far off.

They drove slowly up one street and down the next: round Hill Rise; and into a square that Holly and Jon called Frog Place, because they had once seen a frog in a garden there. As they went past that very house, Holly screamed, "There he is!"

It wasn't a frog she saw this time. It was Jon.

When he left Hill Top he had run and run till he found himself close to Frog Place. So then he stopped running, and went to that house to see if the frog might still be there.

He looked over the low garden wall. He couldn't see the frog; but he saw something else—low down by the front door, there was a cat-door, a small square flap like a letter-box in the house wall.

As Jon looked, a fat white cat bounced out of the cat-door and sat down on the path, licking her paws. Behind her the little door shut with a sharp click: but it didn't stay shut. It went click-click, click-click, as though it were blowing in a strong wind—only there was no wind today.

Then, as Jon gazed, first a tiny white paw came under the flap, and next, a tiny pink nose; there was a great heave, and out through the door staggered a small white kitten. It wobbled over to its mother and sat by her on the path.

By that time Jon was inside the garden, sitting down on the path to stroke them both. But still the cat-door went click-click; and before long he saw a tiny black paw, and a pink and black nose, and out came a black kitten to sit with the others. Soon there were five kittens, three white and two black, chasing their tails in the sun. And then the cat-door stayed shut, and made no more clicks.

So, when Miss Tee and Holly jumped out of the car, he looked up at them, all smiles, and said to Holly, "Look!" And to Miss Tee, "Don't you

think we need a kitten at Hill Top? We can call it Froggie. And—could we have a proper kitten-door, like that?"

Holly felt so glad he was safe, and so wild with rage at him, for giving her such a fright—she didn't know whether to hug him or hit him first.

That was how they found themselves, on this queer Friday afternoon, sitting in Miss Tee's room at Hill

Top, drinking tea and eating delicious yellow cake, to make up to all three of them for having missed dinner.

Miss Tee took the cake from a smart zip-up shopping bag. Cutting it into slices, she said:

"My mother asked me to buy this for her. Wasn't it lucky? I can get her another on my way home——"

Her mother! Holly and Jon stared in surprise, and Miss Tee laughed.

"Oh yes! You're not the only ones with a busy mother at home. And", she added, sipping her tea, "my mother doesn't like to be kept in the dark about things, either. Well, who does? So I think I must come and see Mrs. Gale, and tell her what's been going on this week."

Jon gazed at her, mute, his slice of cake in his paw. Miss Tee went on very kindly:

"Jon. I'm glad you've been happy with us. But you're going to like Park Road School just as much."

Still he looked at her, and said nothing.

"Oh, yes, you are! Eat your cake. I promise. I won't tell you *why*—not now. But on Monday, after school, I shall call to see you and Mother. And then I'll tell you."

So it was all settled. On Monday, Jon was to go to his proper school at last. On Monday afternoon, at four o'clock, Mother would hear all about his misdeeds. No wonder he looked grave.

But Miss Tee pressed more cake on them, and filled up their cups, and let them help each other to lumps of sugar with little silver sugar-tongs which her mother had given her. Then she said:

"Off with you now. No more school today. Run and play in the park, till it's time to go home."

As they went out, past the buzzing class-rooms, Holly spoke. "Never mind. There's all of Saturday and Sunday first."

Jon nodded. They set off down the hill, running and skipping.

Passing the church hall, they had to stop to let some people go by: four of them, carrying large cardboard boxes of clothes from a car to the hall. A red poster on the door said, "Jumble Sale. Saturday. 2 p.m. sharp."

"Race you to the park," said Jon.

But Holly stood still, looking after one of those boxes. Right on top of a pile of hats, she had seen —a black velvet riding-cap.

TEN

A ride to the rescue

Saturday morning was busy for all the Gales. Dad took over the shop, Mother did her own shopping, and Holly and Jon had jobs to do, before they went out to play.

This Saturday, Holly woke up with her head full of plans.

First, she meant to slip off after breakfast and take a bus to Wild Apple Gate and have a ride. Then, by two o'clock, she must be at the church hall for that jumble sale. . . .

She got up at once to lay the breakfast. Washing up, of course, must wait. Her other job was to make her own bed and Jon's. She woke him by pulling off all the covers. He slid to the floor, dragging them with him, and lay there snoring. She fetched two cold wet flannels from the bathroom to help wake him. That led to a pillow fight, and Mother called:

"What on earth is going on?"

Holly called back meekly, "I'm making the beds."

"So I can hear. What's Jon doing?"

From across the room, Jon made his frog-face at Holly. She saw her chance and flung the dripping flannels again, one after the other. They landed on his face, *splish-splash*.

"He's washing," said Holly.

At breakfast he got his own back. Holly ate her egg and toast at top speed, and began to clear plates and mugs to wash up, almost before they were empty. Dad and Mother were in a hurry too, so they didn't mind: they took the hint, and soon went away. But Jon clung to his things for more toast, more milk, an apple, bread and jam . . . Holly felt she had never been so cross with him since the day he was born.

"What jobs have you got?" she asked.

"Helping Dad in the shop."

"Get on, then. Give me your mug, quick."

"I don't have to be quick. It's Saturday."

"You *do*. Give it here. Let go, I tell you."

Jon let go too fast and the mug crashed. Jon wept. It was his rabbit mug: an old friend. Holly had to fetch him 30 pence to get a new one from the china shop.

He cheered up at once and asked, "Where did you get all that money?"

"I robbed a bank. Go on, hurry, Dad will be after you . . ." She pushed him out of the door.

Now she could get away. She put the broken bits of mug in a paper bag and dropped them into the litter bin at the bus-stop. Then she had a long, long wait for the right bus. Jon would be coming to play in the park. He mustn't see her there. Hurry, bus, hurry. . . . It came at last.

By the time she jumped off at Wild Apple **Gate**, all the morning's fuss and flurry seemed far away. Up here on the moor she felt carefree and happy. It was a wild windy day, with low grey clouds speeding in the sky. Leaves flew about like yellow birds. The robin's thin little song blew away as he sang.

She came to the shop and tried the door handle.

It didn't open the door. She tried again. Then she saw a white card: CLOSED. OPEN AT 12.

At *twelve*? For a moment it seemed to mean, Open At Midnight. She gave a shiver. It would be queer up here in the middle of the night, with the dark lonely moor all round, and a moon in the clouds, and owls hooting. No time for pony rides: broom-stick rides might be more likely. That old lady would make a good witch, with her thistle-down hair, and bright brown eyes, and her black cat.

> *Leap, fox; hoot, owl; wail, warbler sweet:*
> *'Tis midnight now's a-brewing;*
> *The fairy mob is all abroad,*
> *And witches at their wooing . . .*

That came from a poem they had read in class. The next verse went:

> *Then sing, lully, lullay, with me,*
> *And softly, lill-lall-lo, love,*
> *'Tis high time, and wild time,*
> *And no time, no, love.*

Then she remembered: it wasn't evening now. It was Saturday morning. So the card just meant 12 noon. Two more hours. Could she wait as long as that? She mustn't be late for dinner, or for the jumble sale.

As she stood there, thinking quickly, she heard a strange kind of noise. Not foxes or owls, and not a fairy mob, either: but *some* kind of mob was making it. She was sure it came from the field: shouts and yells, and whistles, and—the thud of ponies' hooves. Someone *must* be having rides, even if the shop were shut.

She hopped over the fence and ran round the tea-room, and down the garden.

She came to the gate. There was no sign of the old lady. But, in the field, three of the ponies were being ridden at a mad gallop, round and round, by yelling boys. Big boys—much older than she was. Their feet came down close to the ground as they sat on Boxer, Prince and Dobbin. Not Lion: he stood alone at the end of the field, watching.

More boys were running and shouting among the ponies. All of them held long sticks, cut from the hedge. The riders were kicking their heels into the ponies' sides, the rest were cutting at them to make them go faster.

As Holly looked, two of the runners made a dart and grab at Lion. He gave a loud snort, threw up his head and dashed to the other side of the field.

Holly looked at that notice by the gate: No racing, galloping or kicking. . . . This was what it meant. The old lady had said that rough boys came here; they had come again, and there was no one to stop them: no one but *her*.

How was she going to do it? She tried to scream, "Stop!" But the wind blew her voice away. It was like a bad dream: she would never make them hear. She would have to go right up to them, and say— well, what? They would never take any notice. But she had to try. She began to climb the gate.

Those two boys were after Lion again, trying to corner him. They had got near; but Lion was far too clever for them. He eyed them coolly, dodged at the last moment, and raced down to the gate.

Then, in a flash, Holly saw what to do.

What else had her friend said, that first day? "We have to keep the gate shut . . . he'll nip through and run off to the farm."

She was sitting on the top bar now. As Lion trotted near, she called softly:

"Coop, coop—come on, Lion, good boy——"

She drew back the iron lever that held the gate. It swung open. Lion stopped, a foot away. Too late, the boys gave an angry yell—they had seen her! But Lion had made a dash for the gap, and got through. Just as he did so, Holly slid from the top bar on to his back.

She hadn't known she could do it, till it was done.

Here she was, on Lion's back, holding on by his mane, then by his neck strap. And they were free!

Uproar broke loose from the mob; but Holly had no time to think of them any more. She could only think of sticking on Lion's back. He was trotting hard: it was clear that he knew where he was going.

A path ran through gorse and heather to a place far off on the edge of the moor, with trees and roofs and stone walls. That must be the farm.

Then to Holly it seemed as though he took off into the air, like a pony with wings. He wasn't trotting any more. He was moving through the air, but his hooves still touched the grass. On and on they went at this flying pace, so smoothly yet so fast. This wasn't like any riding she had done so far. Then she knew: Lion was cantering.

And it was heaven.

Holly had been in a swing-boat at a fair, and on

a rocking-horse, and in a real boat on the sea. It was a bit like all these; yet, really, not like any of them, but far better. She wasn't in the least afraid. She felt that she could go on for ever like this, and never get tired, never fall off. . . .

She sang to herself, "Now I really *am* riding."

At that moment, Lion saw his master coming from the farm. The next moment, Holly wasn't really riding, but really flying through the air. Lion had pulled up short, with a shrill whinny. She went on, over his head, to land with a gasp at the farmer's feet.

She fell on soft grass. She wasn't hurt: only surprised. It had been so sudden. She sprang up and found herself looking into a dark, angry face. The farmer growled:

"What's this? Who let Lion out? Who said you could ride him?"

Holly cried, "Oh, come quick. Please. Those boys—up there in the field—they're hurting the ponies——"

The farmer didn't waste time asking any more questions. He grabbed Holly with one hand and Lion with the other, and made for the farm, shouting as he went, "Hi there! Tom! Len! Keeper!"

Two men and a dog came running. Holly knew the dog: he was the one she'd seen in the shop. Then all five of them were in a van, and the farm gate was shut on Lion, and the van was bumping up a cart track to the top of the moor.

When the boys saw the van they took to their heels and ran, some one way, some the other. Men and dog were after them: the farmer shouted back to Holly: "Wait there!"

But Holly didn't wait.

For, as the culprits ran off, she saw one of them clearly, for the first time. And she knew him: one of the paper-boys from the shop. Had he seen *her?* He'd know her, she was sure. If the men were to catch him, and bring him back to the van, she would be in trouble too. He would tell Mother she'd been here, perhaps. And that would be the end of her secret pony rides.

She looked round. Far away over the moor a bus was coming. Holly ran for it.

And now for the jumble sale . . .

"At 2 p.m. sharp" the doors of the hall were flung open, and Holly was first inside.

She made a bee-line for the hat stall, but for one chilling moment she couldn't see the black velvet cap. Then she spied it, right at the back of the stall, and spoke up with a gasp of relief: "That one, please."

Then she saw the label: 10p, it said: and, under that: SOLD.

The stall-holder said, "Oh dear. I'm sorry, love. That's taken for the youth club rag. Dick Turpin's Ride, they're doing."

Then she looked more closely at Holly's crest-fallen face.

"Did you want it for dressing-up, dear? Won't something else do?"

"No, I—I wanted—I meant to go riding . . ."

"Really riding?" The lady took this in slowly. "On a horse?" she asked, wide-eyed, as though she'd said, "On a *moose*?"

"Yes," Holly gulped, turning away.

The good soul called her back.

"Here, you grab it quick, love, while my back's turned—I can make one for the club, I dare say. Pop it in this bag——"

Holly paid ten pence, gave her a beaming smile and fled from the hall with her prize.

ELEVEN

"Promise not to look"

On Sunday it was Jon's turn to wake early, with a plan in his head.

Tomorrow, there would be the new school, with new class-mates, new teachers, new everything. And without Puffball.

He saw that he would have to go, this time. But he must see Puffball once more, and wave to her from the gate, and tell her he would be back sometimes.

It was easy to slip out after dinner. Dad was reading the paper. Mother and Holly were in the kitchen, talking about a new jersey Mother was going to knit for Holly.

"Yellow," he heard Holly say. "With a polo neck. Like people wear to go riding." And Mother laughed: "Now, why——?"

Jon tiptoed out of the door and down the stairs.

Again, he was lucky at Hill Top. The school keeper was there, giving food and water to the animals. So the school gate was open; and so was the wire run.

He had some crisps in his pocket for Puffball, and a brussels sprout. But he couldn't see her anywhere at first.

The keeper went off to the back of the school, to fill a bucket. Jon saw his chance and skipped in through the door of the run. A new hutch stood by itself in a corner. He peered in. There she was: half hidden in a great nest of straw, like a tiny white toy in a packet of corn flakes.

She didn't come out when he spoke to her; she peeped from the nest, then snuggled deeper into the straw.

"But you're all alone!" he said aloud. "Why have they put you here by yourself? Poor little Puffball! Shall I let you out?"

The keeper was still out of sight. He looked at the empty playground, the munching rabbits, the nibbling mice: *they* wouldn't tell tales. He said again:

"You don't like being alone, do you?" His hand stole to the hutch door. He whispered, "Like to come and stay with me? Just for one night?"

Then—had he really torn off his pullover, lifted Puffball out of her nest, rolled her snugly in the pullover, shut the hutch, slid out of the wire run, out of the playground, off and away?

He must have done all that. For there he was, half-way down the hill, walking slowly now, hugging his bundle.

"They'll think you've been kidnapped!" he whispered. "But I've only borrowed you. It wasn't fair, leaving you by yourself."

Turning into Park Road, he added, "I'll take you back in the morning, first thing. No one will ever know—I expect."

At the door of the flat he stopped to listen. Mother and Dad were talking now, in the sitting-room. So where was Holly? Still in the kitchen? He must risk it. He tiptoed down the passage to their bedroom.

Safe! It was empty.

He shut the door softly, sat on the floor and unrolled the pullover. He began to stroke Puffball and talk to her in a whisper. All the time, he wanted to shout and sing. For a whole day he would have a pet of his own, after all.

Now he must hide her. The toy box would be safest.

The box stood beside his bed. He put Puffball under his quilt, and threw all the toys out on to the rug. He made a soft nest in the box, with woolly vests, socks and jerseys from his own drawer. He went to the bathroom, still on tiptoe, to fetch water in a clean glass ashtray. Then he had a bright idea:

he took a large roll of cotton wool from the bathroom shelf, tore off the blue paper and fluffed the
cotton wool into a great warm cloud. When he put
her in, she began to burrow under the white cloud,
out of sight.

He gave her the crisps and the brussels sprout,
and propped the box lid open a little way with his
toy sword, so that she would have air.

He'd been so busy, he had not heard anyone
open the door. But when he stood up again, Holly
was standing there. He began slinging his toys into
the cupboard, trying to look cool and calm. But
his heart beat fast.

Holly said in a fierce whisper, "Look out! What are you doing?"

She ran across to the cupboard, took out a large brown paper bag from the shelf where he was throwing the toys, and held it with both hands, just as he'd been holding Puffball a minute ago. *Had* she seen anything?

They glared at each other. She said again, "What are you doing? All your stuff, all over my room——"

"It's my room too. I'm playing."

He couldn't help stealing a look at the box. She was on to him in a flash. "You're up to something. What's in there?"

He stood in front of the box and began to plead. "Don't look. Don't. It's a secret." She pushed him. He made a snatch at the paper bag. That was a lucky move. She shrieked, "Don't touch!"

He had hold of it. The paper split a little and he saw something black inside, before she got it away. She hissed, "Don't you dare touch. It's *my* secret."

They eyed each other, simmering, like two cats on a wall.

"All right then," Jon said. "If you promise not to look, I will, too."

"*I* know. You're playing you've got a pet guinea pig!"

Jon went white. But then he saw that she hadn't

really found out. She just thought it was a game. She turned to the cupboard, laid the bag on a higher shelf and said, "Leave that alone. Promise not to to look?"

It was a long day. Jon found out again—as he'd begun to find that week at Hill Top—that it is one thing to get what you want, by hook or by crook; and quite another thing to enjoy it, at least as much as you'd hoped.

He was afraid to leave the bedroom in case Puffball might squeak. By good luck, again, it came on to rain hard, so no one said, "Come on out for a nice walk." He spread his toy farm on the floor in case Dad or Mother looked in. Most of the time he spent just sitting by the box—glad she was there, hoping nothing would go wrong. . . .

At bedtime he was "on pins" for fear Puffball might squeal or rustle, and give away the secret to Holly. But she made no sound at all. He'd never known her so quiet; and she hadn't eaten anything. Had she enjoyed her visit? A pity it must be over so soon.

He lay in bed, when the light was out, going over and over the plan for the morning. He must be sure to wake at first light—before even the paper-boys came—and smuggle her out of the flat, up to Hill

Top. It wasn't going to be easy. How could he get her back into that hutch? He'd have to wait for the school keeper, and watch for his chance, as he'd done this afternoon. The keeper would be there early, he was sure. It would work out all right: so long as he woke in time. He *must* do that. Five o'clock, even: or six?

But when Holly opened her eyes, at half-past seven on Monday morning—Jon was still fast asleep.

TWELVE

In the box

The sound of the front door woke Holly. That must be Dad, off to work.

Holly went to wash. When she came back, she saw that Jon was awake now; but he hadn't moved. His eyes looked big and dark, his face small and pale, over the sheet. Odd, he looked: as though he'd had a fright.

Mother was at the door. "Buck up, Jon. You'll be late."

He gave a little moan.

"Jon! What's the matter?"

He spoke in a whimper. "I can't get up."

Mother came to his bedside. "Now, Jon. I've got your breakfast ready. Egg and beans. Come along."

"I don't want any. I feel sick. I can't get up."

Holly asked, "Is it one of your tummy aches?"

"Yes! That's what it is! Oh, oh——"

Mother said, "We must get the doctor."

"No!" He stopped moaning. "I don't want the doctor. I just want to stay here . . ."

In the end Holly went off to school alone, with a note to the Head, saying Jon was ill. She *must* have that, she said, or *she* wouldn't go either. . . . Poor Mother sighed.

The minute he was alone, he hopped out of bed, knelt by the box and lifted the lid.

What he saw then made him gasp and sob: "Oh! Oh! Oh!"

This time, the sobs were real.

Mother came in a hurry. He hadn't known she was so near. He dived back into bed: but he couldn't stop wailing.

"Is it so bad? I'm going to ring the doctor."

"No!" He sat up and clutched her. "I'm not crying because of the tummy ache. I'm crying because —because—because I've got to miss school!"

For the first time that morning, Mother laughed.

"Well! That's a new tune, I must say. Now drink this."

"This" was a fizzy drink of warm water. Glad it was no worse, he drank it down. The shop bell rang. Mother drew the curtains and left him.

Jon lay staring at the wall. What was he to do now? What had he *done*?

He couldn't look in the box again.

When he first woke, and knew that he had overslept, his idea had been to wait till the others were out of the way—Mother in the shop, Holly at

school—and then rush to Hill Top and give back his borrowed guest. Of course it would mean awful trouble: they must have missed her by now. But they would have been glad to get her back.

Then, as soon as he'd looked in the box, he knew he couldn't do that any more. This was real trouble: as real as his own panic-stricken sobs.

What was going to happen to him? The school keeper had seen him: he would tell Miss Tee. She would soon guess his name, even if the keeper didn't know it. Then what——?

They would think he was a thief: he had stolen Puffball. They might tell the police.

Jon never forgot that dreadful day. Every time the shop bell rang, far away down the stairs, he held his breath.

Still no one came for him.

It was very odd: but, in spite of all this fright and worry, by noon he was so hungry he could have eaten three school dinners, one after the other. Better not tell Mother that: she might say he was well enough for afternoon school. . . . Well, why not?

No. He must stay where he was, and think what to do. But what *could* he do, *now*?

Mother came in with a cup of thin soup and two dry biscuits on a plate. He did a little moaning—but not too much, in case she spoke of the doctor again—and sat up to nibble and sip. He tried not to think of last Monday's dinner, sausage toad, and plums and custard; or to think of the box and what lay in it.

The afternoon was long and terrible. At last Holly came in from school. She put her head round the door and whispered, "Jon?"

He lay still, his eyes shut. Should he ask her to help? Still he couldn't make up his mind.

He heard her come in on tiptoe, and steal to the cupboard to take out something. That paper bag, it must be. Peering through his eyelids, he saw her at the glass, trying on something black. Some kind of hat. Then she must have put it back in the bag: he heard a rustle. Next, there was the sound of a drawer sliding open, and the chink of money.

The front-door bell rang.

Jon sprang up in bed, his eyes wide open. Holly

98

stood in the middle of the room, holding the bag. They looked at each other and gasped, at the same time—"Miss Tee!"

They'd both forgotten all about her visit. Jon cried in panic, "Don't let her come in! I don't want to see her!"

Holly slid the paper bag under her bed and went to listen at the door.

"They're coming upstairs!"

The door of the flat was open now. Jon could hear voices and footsteps. He knew two of the voices: Miss Tee, of course, and Mother. But there was a third he didn't know. A man's voice. He felt cold all over. His blackest fear had come true. They knew he'd stolen Puffball.

"Listen!" Holly was still at the door. "Who's that man?" She giggled. "Do you think it's Miss Tee's *grandfather*?"

When she looked round Jon was out of bed. He began to get dressed.

"Did Mother say you could get up?"

"He's come for me," said Jon, his face white. He sat down to put on his socks.

"Who's come? Whatever for? Oh—is it the doctor?"

"No," he said, quite cool now. "It's a copper." He scuffed into his slippers, adding, "Come on. I've got to get it over."

They were there in the sitting-room: Miss Tee, looking grave; Mother, a bit puzzled, her mind half in the shop—she must have left someone down there to look after things; and a man, in plain clothes, standing by the fire.

Jon and Holly stood still in the doorway. Mother began, "Oh, Jon. What have you been doing?"

He said nothing: he just stared, first at Miss Tee, so pale and quiet, and then at the man. It was Holly who spoke. She took one look at him too, and burst out:

"But that's not a p'liceman. He's our new science master!"

Mother laughed. "Oh, come. Of course he's not a policeman!" And the young man smiled.

But Miss Tee didn't smile.

He said to Jon, "Yes. Hello. I hear you're a very keen zoologist."

"He's *what*?" asked Holly, before she could stop herself. And Mother said, "He may be. I'm afraid he's also a very naughty boy—going to the wrong school!"

The science master went on, as though he hadn't heard: still talking to Jon himself, in a man-to-man sort of way.

"It's a good thing you're coming to Park Road now. Because we're going to keep animals too. Starting this term. So you can help me look after them—will you?"

Jon looked at him; and then he looked at Miss Tee. Still she hadn't smiled or spoken; and still she looked grave.

Now she said, "Yes. Park Road *were* going to start off with two baby guinea pigs. From Hill Top. Puffball was due to have a family. But I'm afraid"—she stopped, and went on slowly—"I hate to tell you this, Jon. But something very sad has happened. Puffball has been stolen."

Jon tried to speak, but he couldn't. Miss Tee added:

"We've only just found out. She was left in a

hutch by herself. And when we looked just now—
she'd gone."

And then Holly gave a cry. "Jon! Is that
what——?" He turned to face her. She stammered,
"—What—what was in the box? *That* was what
made you ill?"

He nodded. She gave a shudder. "Oh, Jon—how
awful. You mean——"

He broke in, "I didn't know till this morning. I
meant to get up early and take her back. And then
I—I—I looked in the box, and I couldn't——"

"You mean," Holly whispered, "she'd died in
the night?"

Jon struggled for words. They came in a great shout. "Died! Of course she hasn't died! But she's in my box, and she—she's gone and had a whole lot of guinea pig kittens. . . ."

THIRTEEN

High time and wild time

Holly sat in the bus, her brown paper bag on her lap. She had got away, after all. It had seemed that she never would—with all that fuss about Puffball.

Still, the fuss had helped her, in the end. At this moment they would still be at it, scolding Jon, and making plans for Puffball and her family.

Jon had told them what a fright he'd had when he found them that morning. Last term, when the mother rabbit had *her* babies—the ones that used to play puss-in-the-corner so cleverly—Miss Brown had warned them that, for the first week or two after they were born, you mustn't go near them; or the mother might kill them.

So he knew he couldn't take the guinea-pig babies back to Hill Top; and he hadn't known what to do next.

The science master said he had been quite right to leave them alone; and the box must stay where it was for the time being. Jon could give Puffball a little food and water, because she was used to him.

And later on—when the babies were out of the nest —he could choose two of them for Park Road School. So everything had come right for Jon.

And Miss Tee said, "There's glory for you."

Boys! thought Holly darkly: they got away with anything.

So she had slipped out, rushed into jeans and caught the bus for Wild Apple Gate.

She had a seat to herself at the back. No one could see her as she opened the bag, drew out her cap, and ran a finger proudly over the soft velvet. The cap was hard inside, like a crash-helmet, to save your head if you fell off the pony. She put it on, did up the chin strap and looked at herself in the bus window. There she was, looking just like Lucy . . .

As she jumped off by the tea-shop, the conductor clicked his tongue at her, the way people do to a pony. Holly laughed; she could hardly get to the field fast enough.

She ran to the shop and turned the door handle.

The door stayed shut, as it had done on Saturday. She shook the handle, tried it again, gave the door a push. No good. The key must be turned. She tried to peer through the glass pane, to see the old lady; but something was in the way.

The blind was down. And there, stuck to the pane, inside, she saw a white card. A new one.

She read it; and stared at it. Her hand dropped from the door handle. She whispered, "It can't be. It can't be!"

The card said: CLOSED FOR WINTER.

Holly looked for the notice about pony rides. It was gone. The paper had been torn off the board. Only a rusty drawing pin was left, and one rag of paper, fluttering in the cold wind.

She stood a moment longer, too stunned to move.

Then she thought—"The ponies!" They might still be in their field. But—what about those boys? It wouldn't be safe any more: the boys might come back.

She sprang over the fence and ran to the field. It was empty. No ponies: nothing. Only sodden grass and brown hedges; not like that green sunny place where she'd been so happy.

Closed for winter.

She went slowly back through the garden. The tea-room was bare, all the tables and chairs gone, too. There was nothing left. She must go home, and put away the riding-cap, and find something else to do.

As she looked through the glass door for the last time, the blind made a looking-glass; she could see her cap again. It was too much. Tears ran down her face and she sobbed:

"Oh, they might have waited! They might have. It's not winter yet. Oh, Dobbin . . . Lion. . . ."

A car was coming along the moor road. She looked away to hide her tears. It was nearly level with the shop; she gave one quick look. The car slowed: the driver had put his brakes on. It stopped, and a voice cried:

"Holly? Holly! Is that you?"

It was Dad.

That was the end of Holly's secret. But, for a long time Dad couldn't make head or tail of her story. It all came out back to front, between sobs, while she sat beside him in the car.

First, he had to hear about the pony rides, now lost to her for ever; at least for the whole winter, which came to the same thing. Then she told about her bus rides from the park; then about the table-laying and Aunt Jinny's pay; and then about the pony children on the beach. . . .

At last, with Dad asking questions, and shaking his head at some of the answers (but laughing here and there, too, she saw) Holly grew calm enough to tell it all again, the right way round: only missing out the part about the green wishbone, which could never be told to anyone; and her ride to the rescue on Saturday, because that was another story, and it could wait.

When she came to the end—to the white card, over there on the door, and the empty field—they both sat quietly for a moment. There might be a row, she saw; but she felt too sad to care.

Then Dad spoke. "Do you know the way to the farm?"

"The *farm*?"

"Where they keep your ponies. On a farm, you said."

"Oh . . . yes. It's down there. You can see the cart track. Why?"

He smiled and started the car; but not to go home. He turned it, drove back along the moor road, then into the farm track. Holly sat speechless.

After a moment, a sudden wild hope made her sit up, scrub at her face with a hanky and set her cap to rights.

Now they were at the farmyard. Still Dad said nothing but, "Hop out." She hopped; and then they were walking over the yard to the farmhouse door, while the dog Keeper came to greet them: not barking, but with a friendly "Woof." He knew her at once.

Just by the yard, there was a paddock, and four ponies grazing in it. She grabbed her father's hand.

"Dad, look! It's *them*—there they are!"

But he was looking at someone else. A man had come out of the door and stood gazing at them, while Keeper frisked at their heels. The farmer.

Before Dad could speak, he flung open the door again, calling to someone inside, "Mother! Come out, will you? Quick! She's here—the little lass. She's come to see us!"

The old lady knitted her way to the door and smiled at Holly, saying:

"I told you she was on her way. I saw you in my tea-leaves," she told Holly, "riding our Lion. Not five minutes gone—and there we'd been asking and asking, and trying to find you, ever since Saturday."

"To find *me*?" Holly stammered.

"To thank you," said the farmer, "for a right smart bit of work."

That was when Dad heard about the ride on Lion. It was the farmer who told it; and Holly broke in to ask:

"Those boys—*did* you catch them?"

"And thumped them," he said shortly.

She drew a deep breath. "Oh, good. So they won't come back?"

His face grew a shade less grim. "We'll see. I told them to come back."

"What!"

He smiled. "Said I'd look out for a horse their size. Then, come the summer, if I can spare the time, I'll teach 'em something better than bully-ragging our ponies. So", he grinned at Dad, "if I don't watch it—next thing, I'll be running a riding school, and no time for my farm."

"Very nice", said the old lady, "that will be."

"Ah! All your doing, this is, Mother. There you sit, looking in your tea-cup, and first you see a tea-shop, and then you see pony rides for the kids. . . . Always a one for the horses, Mother was."

His mother looked across at Holly: "I still am," she said. "And here's another, just the same."

Dad got a word in at last.

"I came to ask you—I found her up there, so upset, seeing you'd closed—but could you let me bring her, now and then, in the winter? Just to see these ponies she's so set on, and give them a bit of sugar. . . ."

"Hold on," said the farmer. "We've a better idea, Mother and me. That's why we were trying to find her . . ."

Their idea was that Holly should come there on Saturday mornings; first to have proper riding lessons from the farmer, and then to ride the ponies—"and lush them up a bit, you know, and keep them in hand for next summer."

Holly felt her head spin. It couldn't be true, she thought. She must be asleep and dreaming. It was like what Miss Tee had said to Jon: "There's glory for you."

". . . And if you've a friend you can bring," the

farmer was saying, "two of you will be twice as useful."

"Oh!" Holly came out of her daze. "I've got a brother—would he do? He—he's a very keen zoologist," she added: in case they thought all boys were rowdy and rough.

"He's *what*?" Dad asked, just as Holly herself had done. And the farmer looked taken aback.

"How old, though? Our ponies are small, don't forget."

"Oh, Jon's small too. He's not even seven yet."

They all laughed; and the farmer said:

"A zoologist will be fine. You bring him along."

The Gales had a lively supper that night. Holly and Jon had never sat up so late, or talked so much.

But they didn't do all the talking. Before they went to bed, Dad told them, "I just want a few words with you two scamps. . . ." He cleared his throat.

"Now then. From what we can make out, Mother and I, you've been having a high old time, this past week. Running wild, the minute our backs were turned. And not so much as a word to us— let alone asking leave. Well: from now on, that's all out. Do you understand?"

And so on, for some time.

High time and wild time, Holly thought. Yes, that was what it had been. Just as the poem said.

Her secret trips up to the moor, the secret pony rides: that time was over and done with now. Already it seemed far away, almost like a dream:

No time, no, love.

Wild Apple Gate wouldn't be the same, with Dad and Jon. Nothing would ever again be quite like that.

But still—you could never tell—the new times might be even better.

FOURTEEN

What came of wishing?

Now the long day was over. They lay in the dark, waiting for sleep. By Jon's bed, safe in her cotton-wool nest, Puffball made a faint rustle.

He whispered, "Did you hear that?"

"Yes."

He turned to and fro on his pillow. "I say, Holly?"

"Mm."

"My wish came true. Just the way I wished it. Did yours?"

"Yes."

"All of it?"

"Yes."

"Was it," Jon breathed, "was it really the wish-bone, do you think?"

Holly was quiet for so long, he thought she must have gone to sleep. At last she whispered:

"I think it was *us*. Partly. We wanted our wishes so much, we *made* them happen."

It was his turn to lie still and think. Then. . . .

"But can you do that? Make your wishes come true?"

"I don't know yet," said Holly. "Let's try to find out."